Rescuing the Preacher

(Christmas Rescue Series)

Cheryl Wright

Copyright

Rescuing the Preacher

(Christmas Rescue Series)

Copyright ©2019 Cheryl Wright

Small Town Romance Publications

Cover Artist: Black Widow Books

This is a work of fiction. Characters, places, and incidents are a figment of the author's imagination.

Any resemblance to actual events, locales, organizations or people living or dead, is totally coincidental.

This book was written by a human and not Artificial Intelligence (A.I.).

This book can not be used to train Artificial Intelligence (A.I.).

Dedication

To Margaret Tanner, my very dear friend and fellow author, for her enduring encouragement and friendship.

To Alan, my husband of almost 50 years, who has been a relentless supporter of my writing and dreams for many years.

To You, my wonderful readers, who encourage me to continue writing these stories. It is such a joy knowing so many of you enjoy reading my stories as much as I love writing them for you.

Table of Contents

Chapter One

Twin Falls, Idaho 1880

Rose Charleston was in despair. Her parents had deemed to marry her off to the town's lawyer.

Yes, he was rich, and was considered to be a great catch. He was also very handsome, there was no doubt about that.

"So what is the problem?" her father had asked when he'd told her the news, as if being forced to marry a man almost double her age wasn't an issue.

At twenty-six she was past her prime marrying age, but to be forced into marriage with a fifty-year-old? It didn't bear thinking about.

Mother waved him away. He always made things worse anyway.

"Rose, dear," Mother said gently. "This is an amazing opportunity. Half the women in town would beg to be in your position." She pursed her lips and Rose knew there was no getting out of it. "Besides, your father has already sealed the deal. You *will* marry Jonas Hanson in two weeks."

"Really, Mother? You made those arrangements without even consulting me?" Rose turned her face away. She was so angry right now, and didn't want to even look at her mother.

"Be nice, Rose! Mr Hanson will be here in a few minutes for supper. Be on your best behavior." Then she stormed out of the room.

Her head was spinning. She didn't want to marry an old man. She wanted someone closer to her own age.

She sighed. At least he was respectable and well-dressed, and he was very likeable too. At least it seemed that way on the few occasions she'd seen him at church.

Some of her friends had been forced into marriage with smelly, nasty old men. She supposed she should be grateful for small mercies, but that didn't mean she wanted to comply with her parent's wishes.

She stared blankly out of her bedroom window. Mother was right, at least half her friends would swap places with her in a heart-beat. To marry the second richest man in town was a dream come true for most spinsters.

But not for Rose.

She wanted the man of her choosing to be her husband. She wanted a marriage built on love, not one of convenience.

She heard mutterings at the front door and her heart skipped a beat. *Was this really happening?*

"Rose! Come down here please." Mother's voice was loud and clear. The last thing she wanted was to face Jonas Hanson, but she had little choice in the matter.

Her forced wedding was forthcoming, and her future planned for her.

She reluctantly fixed her hair and splashed cold water on her face, endeavoring to remove some of the heat. Rose pushed her hands down her expensive gown to straighten out some of the wrinkles. Why she bothered she didn't know. The last thing she wanted was for Jonas Hanson to find her attractive.

But of course it was already too late.

She slowly, tentatively, made her way down the stairs. He stared up at her, a grin on his face. His tailor-made suit was cut superbly, and his shoes shone. His black hair sat at the edge of his collar.

He was as handsome as she'd remembered from their distant acquaintance.

But she still didn't want to marry him.

"Rose, my dear. You look positively lovely." His hand outreached, he helped her down the last steps. As if she needed anyone's help.

She sighed.

"I'm looking forward to our marriage. You are such a beauty. Why some young man hasn't snapped you up before this, I'll never know."

She squinted at him. She could ask the same. If he was such a catch, why did he remain unmarried at fifty? Did other women know something she didn't? Was he abusive behind doors? A deviant? Or something else entirely?

She flinched when he put his hand to the small of her back. He stared at her and frowned. "Is everything alright, Rose?"

She forced a false smile to her face. "Everything is perfectly fine, thank you Mr Hanson."

He stiffened. "You must call me Jonas, since we are to marry very soon."

She nodded. Rose needed to prepare herself for the inevitable.

"I will send the dressmaker around tomorrow to measure you for your wedding dress. You will have nothing but the best." He lifted her hand and kissed it.

"What if I don't want to marry you," she asked softly. So softly her parents didn't hear. She stared into his eyes and waited for his response.

His whole demeanor changed and his face stiffened. "You will marry me, Rose," he said through gritted teeth. "It was arranged some time ago."

And there it was – a snippet of his true character shone through.

She was shocked at the sudden change in him, but realized she probably shouldn't be.

He nudged her roughly toward the table, then leaned in close to her ear. "Let's have no more of this talk, and enjoy a cheerful night with your parents." He grinned at her as though he'd made a joke. It was all for her parent's sake, of course.

It was difficult, but she smiled at him. Inwardly she was screaming. She had to find a way out of this arranged marriage or she was doomed.

* * *

Dalton Springs, Montana, 1880

"Papa! Papa!"

Preacher Matthew Barnabas was tired.

After contracting pneumonia while still recovering from childbirth, his wife Alice struggled to survive, then finally succumbed.

His parishioners had been wonderful. The women of the town had been especially amazing. They'd taken turns caring for his two children for what seemed forever.

In reality it was probably three months. Perhaps a little more.

Their generosity was beyond all expectations, but he couldn't allow it to continue. And now he was in a bind.

How did one man raise two young children and also tend to his parishioners?

"Papa!"

Grace was becoming impatient – he could hear it in her voice. For a three-year-old, she was certainly feisty. She took after her mother that way.

Dear Alice – how he missed her.

Her smile lit up a room the moment she stepped into it. And she was always willing to lend a helping hand, no matter what.

His heart was empty since she'd passed, his existence meaningless. They had been so much in love, and had she not died, Matthew was certain they would grow old together.

He shook his head. He couldn't afford to think too much on what was done. Alice wouldn't want him to continue mourning her death either. She'd want him to take care of their children, and move forward, he knew she would.

Matthew sighed. He would if only he knew how.

"Papa," Grace said, hands on her hips. "Did you not hear me? I need my hair braided. I cannot do it myself."

He reached for the brush but knew his braiding skills were far from perfect. His children deserved better, but right this minute, he wasn't sure how to do that.

"Ow! Papa, that hurts!"

"I'm sorry, Grace," he said, not meaning to hurt his small daughter. This was not something he was ever meant to do.

He had just finished fixing his daughter's hair when five-month-old Clara began to wail. He supposed it was time to feed her.

Before Alice's untimely death, his work day would be starting about now. He would be preparing for the early morning service, then later visit those parishioners who were shut-ins and unable to attend the church.

He'd since had to cancel morning services, and take the children with him for visitations. The majority of his parishioners didn't mind. In fact, they said it was delightful having little ones visit them.

He supposed it brightened their otherwise dull day.

As for morning services, he hoped to one day restore them.

Clara wailed even louder, breaking into his thoughts. "I'm coming Clara," he called, knowing the child's diaper would be saturated. It always was when she awoke.

Now dry but hungry, he headed toward the kitchen with the baby in his arms. He looked down into her innocent little face. It was like looking into his dead wife's face, and his heart hitched.

He swallowed hard. Matthew wasn't sure how he could do this. He couldn't envisage himself doing this over and over for the months to come, let alone the years he knew he needed to dedicate to raising his two girls.

It was something he needed to think on. One thing he did know – he couldn't continue down this path. He was exhausted within minutes of waking up, and still had a full day ahead of him.

He couldn't contemplate giving up his position as preacher. He loved doing God's work. Besides, what would he do to support his young family?

He'd been a preacher for as long as he could remember. At thirty-four, he was too old to learn something new.

* * *

Chapter Two

"You look bored, Rose."

Rose sat in the parlor, with nothing else to do. The dressmaker had been and taken her measurements, and had shown her a number of gorgeous material samples.

She'd never seen such beautiful fabrics in her life. They outshone anything she'd ever had. And she'd always had the best available.

It was true she'd been spoiled throughout her short life, her parents being what was considered reasonably wealthy. Not as wealthy as Jonas Hanson of course, but they were certainly highly respected.

"Here," Mother said, passing the newspaper to her. "Read this. At least it will give you something to do."

What did she have to lose? She was not allowed to take a job, since that would look bad for her father – as though he'd forced her, which wouldn't be true.

Nor was she allowed to do anything around the house – that's what servants were for. Neither was she allowed to do volunteer work, because of course, that was beneath her.

She hated sitting around doing nothing. Hated it with a vengeance. She might as well read the newspaper. Perhaps she might learn something new.

She rolled her eyes.

Rose snatched up the paper and took it to the table. "Thank you, Mother," she said quietly. "I am beyond bored today."

That was partially true, mostly she was trying to find a way of getting out of her pending marriage.

Spreading the newspaper out on the table, she turned page after page, not finding anything of particular interest. "Did you know Pastor Green is retiring in a couple of months?" she asked her mother.

Mother looked up, rather uninterested. "Yes, I did my dear. It's the reason your wedding was brought forward. We didn't want a stranger marrying you."

The irony in that statement wasn't missed by Rose, but she nodded affably and continued to turn the pages.

"The church picnic is on in two weeks. Can we go, Mother?"

Mother glanced up at her, a frown on her face. "You'll be on your honeymoon. But Father and I will probably attend."

Honeymoon? It wasn't even something Jonas had discussed with her. Would all decisions be taken out of her hands? Would she be nothing but a token wife to carry on his arm?

She felt her anger rise, and tried to damp it down. Rose was an independent thinking young woman. She hated to think that would be taken away from her.

She continued to troll the pages of the oversized newspaper, and finally she came to the advertisements.

Not that she expected anything would catch her eye. She wanted for nothing, except perhaps a man to love her for who she was. Not a husband who was forced on her.

Her eyes zoomed in on a tiny advertisement in a bold black box.

Help Needed. Housekeeping and child-minding required. Board and lodgings provided. Location Dalton Springs, Montana. Contact M. Barnabas.

Rose's heart thudded. It wasn't perfect by any means – she'd never kept house, nor had she had contact with children. But if it meant getting out of marriage to Jonas Hanson, then so be it.

There was a down-side, she realized. The wedding ceremony was in less than two weeks. It wasn't enough time to post a letter and get a response. It would be far too late by that time.

Her eyes downcast, she knew she was defeated. Rose had no choice but to marry a man she barely knew and didn't particularly like.

She memorized the details anyway, deciding to mull it over and hopefully come up with a solution. Rose closed the newspaper and returned it to her mother in the same condition she received it.

"I'm going to lay down for a spell," she said quietly.

Mother's head shot up. "Do you feel poorly, dear?"

Rose sighed. "Yes Mother, I do." She turned tail and stormed up the stairs.

She kicked off her shoes and lay down on the bed. Sleep was elusive, but finally she succumbed. It seemed not long after, her eyes suddenly fluttered open, an idea forming in her mind.

A smiled crossed her lips, and Rose finally knew what she must do. If she didn't plan it fully, she would be thwarted, and that was the last thing she wanted – or needed.

* * *

Rose slipped quietly out of the house in the early hours of the morning.

She filled her carpetbag with as much of her clothing as she could. She knew it was wrong, but raided Mother's cookie jar and took the few notes placed there for a rainy day. To her knowledge, that day had never come.

Right now it was her version of a rainy day. It was dark and full of doom, and that money would be her ticket out of here. Literally.

Rose had no money of her own, and having to steal from her mother didn't sit well with her.

She had decided to steal away in the middle of the night and catch the early train to Dalton Springs. She would be well gone before anyone even woke up.

The small amount in the cookie jar was enough to buy a ticket and perhaps feed her for the trip. She really had no idea what the cost of food would be. She'd never had to buy a thing in her life.

Her heart thudded, and she swallowed hard. *Was she really going to do this?*

Determined, she slipped quietly down the stairs and headed for the front door. Rose stopped as she heard movement behind her.

"Miss Rose," a quiet voice said. She was startled and her heart was pounding in her chest at being caught.

She slowly turned and the butler she'd known her entire life stood watching her keenly. He was in his night apparel and stood tall, as he always did.

Rose reached for the front door. "You didn't see me," she said quietly.

"See what?" he asked. He winked then closed the door quietly behind her.

It was pitch black outside. Rose had never been out at this time. There were a few street lamps burning, but none near her home.

The cold weather had already set in. Soon it would be far worse. She dragged her coat tighter around herself.

She heard footsteps behind her and turned, startled once more. Only this time she felt faint, she was so terrified.

"Miss Rose," that same familiar voice called from behind her.

She sighed with relief. "Oh, it's you, Martin. What are you doing here?" she said with her hands to her heart.

The butler stared at her. "You can't walk the streets alone at this hour. I am here to escort you to the station. Be assured, I will not divulge your secret."

His word was good, she knew. He was loyal for sure, but did that loyalty extend to her parents too?

As if he could read her thoughts he spoke again. "I'll escort you but won't go with you to buy the ticket. I don't want to know where you are going – if I don't know, I can't tell." He winked at her, and she knew he was right.

They hurried to the station – her train would leave in less than half an hour. Rose couldn't afford to miss it. If she did, she wasn't certain she'd have the courage to do this all again.

"Keep your carpetbag close, and don't talk to any strangers, especially men." He moved into to hug her. "Do you have any money?" He was concerned about her, bless him, and pulled out his wallet. "I have a few dollars to spare."

"I have a little. Enough for a ticket and some food." She showed him and he shoved a couple of notes into her hand.

"That won't be enough, Miss Rose, trust me. Take care." He pulled her in and hugged her close. "Please be careful, wherever you go, and whatever you are doing."

She thanked him, and reluctantly moved out of his arms, then headed to the ticket office. Ticket in hand she headed for the platform. When she looked back, Martin had gone.

No doubt he would be grilled in the morning. He might even lose his job if his complicity was discovered.

She hoped for his sake he didn't.

* * *

Rose slowly opened her eyes. She'd lost count of the number of days she'd been on this wretched contraption. Two days? Three? It could even be more.

She felt ill from the constant rocking, and her entire body ached from the uncomfortable seats. She'd taken Martin's advice and held her carpetbag the entire trip, not letting it go for even moments.

She alighted at two of the larger stations and purchased food to sustain her for the rest of the trip. Thankful for Martin's foresight and additional money, as she would have run out before now otherwise.

Upon purchasing her ticket she'd discovered Dalton Springs was too small to have it's own train station, so she'd need to transfer to a stagecoach for the last leg of the trip.

Her biggest hope was the seats were padded. How she wished she'd carried her pillow with her! Even at the risk of looking silly.

She glanced up as a shadow fell over her. "Tickets please." The conductor came to check her ticket for what would be at least the tenth time, perhaps more. With passengers coming and going, it was a constant interruption. One she didn't savor.

"Thank you, Miss." He tipped his hat and was on his way.

She closed her eyes again, and it didn't seem very much later she heard an announcement as the conductor moved along the aisles. "Little Rock. Little Rock."

Rose slowly opened her eyes then began to nod off again, but sensed someone standing over her. "Miss. Miss." He touched her shoulder and Rose stiffened. "Miss, this is your stop."

It was the conductor again. "You need to change here for Dalton Springs. The stagecoach is over there," he said pointing. "It leaves in fifteen minutes."

"Thank you," she said, her heart finally slowing. "I appreciate it." And she did. If she'd missed her stop she'd be stranded. She only had enough money left for the stagecoach, and nothing more.

Rose stretched herself out as she stood. The conductor stood in front of her, no doubt waiting for a tip, but she had none to give.

He eventually moved on.

Clutching her carpetbag, Rose strode toward the stagecoach. She couldn't afford to miss it. This town, Little Rock, lived up to its name. From what she could see there was nothing more than a mercantile, a barber's shop, a blacksmith's shop, and of course, a church.

She hoped Dalton Springs was larger.

She no sooner had the thought than she dismissed it. She was on the run, hiding, and beggars certainly couldn't be choosers. She would accept whatever hand she was dealt in her new locality.

The stagecoach looked sturdy enough, and she climbed up with assistance. It was clearly meant for four adults, but six of them were packed inside.

"That's it," the driver told them. "The rest of you will have to wait for the next coach in about an hour.

Relieved she'd hurried from the train, Rose sat back, enjoying the comfortable seats. At least they were more comfortable than the train, but would she still feel that way after two hours in this new contrivance?

One thing she did know; she would be very pleased to sleep in a real bed tonight.

She sighed. At least her ordeal was nearly ended. *Only two more hours* she told herself over and over, hoping to reduce her fatigue and talk herself into feeling better.

"This is exciting," a rather plump woman with red curls told her. "I've never been in a stagecoach before."

Rose glanced at her. "Neither have I. Are you going to Dalton Springs too?" Not that she was really interested, she was simply being polite.

The woman looked her up and down. "No dear, I'll alight much earlier than that."

Was that meant to be derogatory? Rose really wasn't sure. She glanced to the opposite side of the coach to see three gents sitting there. They all sat tall in their grey suits with perfectly matched ties. She wondered where they were going, but didn't dare ask.

To her left was another woman. This one looked as though she'd rather be anywhere but here. Her chin stood high as if in an act of defiance, and she glanced at the gent sitting directly opposite. "This is already incredibly uncomfortable, George," she said haughtily. "Was there really no other option?"

"None," he said firmly.

Rose watched the exchange and knew her mother would be the same. She'd rather buy out the entire stagecoach than be crammed in like this. She blinked the thoughts away. The last thing she wanted was to fill herself with emotion and make a spectacle of herself in front of all these strangers.

She wanted to clutch her carpetbag as a way to comfort herself, but it had been taken away from her. No luggage was allowed in the coach itself, she was told. And that was that.

Settling herself as best she could, Rose closed her eyes, and didn't open them again until the next stop where the two single gents alighted. The snobbish woman moved to sit beside her husband, giving them all more space. "Thank goodness for that, George," she said with a sigh.

Rose couldn't help but smile when a rather large gent joined them, choosing to sit next to the couple.

It seemed like forever before she arrived at her destination, but Rose was well ready to leave. Between the rocking, the dust, and the complaints from the snobbish woman, she couldn't wait to alight.

The driver helped her down the wonky steps, then passed her luggage, leaving her then to her own devices. As the coach pulled away, she examined her surroundings.

What she hoped to become her new home wasn't a lot bigger than Little Rock, but enough to say it was the biggest of the two.

She could see the mercantile, a bakery, dressmaker, sheriff's office, and a small bank. The church steeple peaked out behind them.

Making her way toward the Mercantile, Rose was sure she would be able to locate M. Barnabas from there. The town was small enough that everyone must surely know all the residents, even if they lived on the outskirts.

She walked slowly up the sidewalk toward her intended destination, and stood outside working up the nerve to go in and make enquiries.

It was then she realized she was in a similar position to a mail order bride. She had arrived at an unknown destination, preparing to meet an unknown employer. She may not be getting married, but she was taking the same sort of risk.

It made her pause.

What if M. Barnabas was an abusive male? She'd assumed the advertisement was written by a woman, simply because of the mention of child-minding. But now she realized that may not be the case at all.

If it wasn't for the fact she'd traveled for many days by both train and stagecoach, she would have turned around right this minute and gone back.

She stopped.

No, she wouldn't do that. She couldn't do that – not unless she was prepared to marry a man who was clearly not what he pretended to be.

She reached out and opened the door. The little bell over the door tinkled and she walked in.

Chapter Three

Grace sat at her father's feet flicking through the pages of a book. Baby Clara sat on his lap.

"Your children are beautiful," Sarah Rogers exclaimed. "Very well behaved too." She dropped her voice to a whisper. "Alice would be so proud."

Tears came to her eyes, and Matthew offered her his kerchief. She brushed it aside. "I'm very sorry, Preacher Barnabas. I don't know what came over me."

He pulled Clara closer. "It is difficult," he said. "For all of us. Our loss was not so long ago. It's sad to think these girls may never remember their mother because of their young ages."

Mrs Rogers sniffed.

Matthew worried his words had set her off again, but she managed to pull herself together. "Tell me, Mrs Rogers. How are things with you now?"

She straightened her shoulders and lifted her chin. "A little better, thank you. The help you arranged for me has made a huge difference. I'm no longer worrying all the time, and have even managed to do a little embroidery. It's something I've missed dearly."

He leaned forward and patted her knee. "That's wonderful. I'm so pleased it helped. Is there anything else I can do for you?"

She grabbed his hand before he could move it away. "If you could say a small prayer for me, I'd be very grateful."

They bowed their heads and prayed together, and he left soon after with his daughters. "I'm so proud of you," he told Grace. "Your behavior was excellent." He was rewarded with a huge grin.

He looked the child over. He'd noticed Mrs Rogers staring at her before they left, but couldn't fathom what she'd found so interesting.

He could see it now, out here in the daylight. The hair he'd braided this morning was falling apart, and her pinafore was inside out. Good gracious!

And he'd paraded the child in front of other parishioners before he'd arrived here. What he was going to do, he had no idea, but the situation was becoming dire. The children needed a woman's hand, but it was an impossible mission.

There was no one suitable in town who was available. The last thing he wanted was to marry so soon after his dear wife's demise.

He would just have to be more vigilant and rise from sleep even earlier than he did now. It would make for a much longer and more difficult day, but he'd do anything for his sweet and innocent daughters.

They headed for home where he would fix Grace's hair once again, and turn her pinafore the right way out. Dear Alice would have had conniptions if she'd seen what he'd done. And out in public no less.

* * *

"I'm looking for M. Barnabas," Rose told the woman behind the counter.

The tiny woman squinted at her. "Joseph!" she called, presumably to her husband.

"Yes, Bertha?" he yelled back.

Her gaze never left Rose's face. "Git out here. There's a strange woman lookin' for M. Barnabas!"

Rose heard his boots hit the floor and he was behind the counter in seconds. He stared at her then looked her up and down.

"Who are you?" His eyes followed her every movement. "And what do you want with *M. Barnabas*?" The name was exaggerated.

She straightened her shoulders and licked her lips. "I…I'm answering an advertisement she placed."

They stared at her, then laughter bubbled up from inside them both. The woman doubled over, she was laughing so much.

Then suddenly they both stopped, and their expressions became serious. "To begin with, *M. Barnabas* is a man," Joseph said.

"An' he's our preacher," Bertha finished for him. "What sort of advertisement?" She squinted at Rose once again. "Show me."

What was she to do? She had no advertisement to show. "It's not really your business," she said, sounding more confident than she felt. "Please tell me where to find him, and I'll go there."

Bertha pursed her lips in an obvious act of defiance.

Joseph on the other hand, wasn't so difficult. "Behind the bakery. Follow the steeple and you'll be there. The cottage is beside the church."

"Thank you, Mr…"

"Stapleton. You can call me, Joseph. Or Joe. Everyone does."

"Thank you, Joe." She spun on her heels and headed for the door.

"See you around, I guess."

Rose nodded. She sure hoped so.

Following Joe's directions, she found the little cottage. It wasn't large, but wasn't tiny either. It had lace curtains in the front windows, and a picket fence with an assortment of flowers out the front.

The garden had been let go, and was full of weeds. Their garden at home was never like that. Then again, they had a gardener who came in twice a week. One day for the flowers, the other for the vegetable patch out back.

Father was stingy and refused to pay for fresh produce when he could grow his own. As if he grew it!

Rose wondered if there was a vegetable patch out the back of the preacher's cottage. She'd never been allowed to potter in the garden, since someone was paid to do that job. What her father hadn't realized was she could have saved him money, had he allowed her.

Not that she knew about plants, but she was willing to learn.

The front door stood wide open and she heard a child scream. "Papa! You're hurting me."

Rose was alarmed.

The wind blew up and a cold breeze hit her. Rose pulled her coat around herself. "Are you cold?" She looked down to see a small girl of three or four, she guessed.

"Only a little." She turned the collar up to warm her neck. "Is Mr Barnabas around?"

Without warning the child was gone. "Papa! There's a strange lady here."

He stood at the end of the hallway and stared. He was tall and trim, and stood in the shadows. He held something in his hands, but she couldn't work out what it was.

"Hello?"

"Mr Matthews?" Once the words were out she remembered his vocation. "Sorry, Preacher Matthews?"

He closed the distance between them. "Yes?"

"My name is Rose Charleston. I'm answering your advertisement."

"Advertisement?"

Rose felt the color drain from her face. She'd traveled all this way and he had no idea what she was talking about. "You advertised for a housekeeper. At least that's what the advertisement said."

It was obvious the man was totally confused. Then suddenly he seemed enlightened. "I didn't do that, but I'll bet I know who did."

Between the travel and the fact she was penniless, not to mention homeless, it was all too much to discover she'd been on a fruitless endeavor with no resolution in sight.

Tears began to fall, and sobs wracked her body. "Oh my dear lady. You must come inside," the preacher told her.

Leading her into the sitting room, he called to the young girl. "Grace, please get Miss Charleston a cup of water from the table." He helped her into a chair.

Rose accepted the water from the small girl. "Here you are."

"Thank you, sweetheart." She stared at her through tears. Grace was a pretty little thing, but rather disheveled. She was well-mannered too.

"Tell me what happened," the preacher said gently. "We'll sort this all out, have no doubt."

Between tears and sobs she relayed the details of the advertisement. Rose explained of her long and arduous trip, and the fact she was now without both money and accommodation.

He listened careful, continuing to hold in his hand the object she'd seen earlier. She wiped the tears from her eyes with the kerchief he offered and finally saw it was a hairbrush.

It made her smile. He followed her gaze. "I was trying to sort out my daughter's hair," he told her gently. "It is far beyond my capabilities."

Grace pulled a face. "He pulls my hair and the braids all fall out," she said with a pout.

"Obviously someone in my parish placed that advertisement. It certainly wasn't me. Although…I certainly could use the help."

Her heart beat picked up. Perhaps she did have a job after all.

He scratched his head. "The problem as I see it," he said quietly. "Is you're an unmarried woman, and I'm an unmarried man. I can't have you live here with me and the children."

She blinked. He didn't have a wife? "What about your wife," she almost whispered.

"Grace, go and check on Clara, would you? That's a good girl." Grace almost danced out of the room, having been given that responsibility. "My wife died some months ago, leaving me to raise the girls alone."

"Oh. I'm very sorry," Rose said, and genuinely meant it.

"I do need help, but I'm not sure how it can be managed. You can't stay here, as I've explained."

"I have no money." She stared down into her hands. "I've used every last coin I had. I can't even buy food."

The enormity of her situation hit her again, and she must have paled as the preacher pushed the water toward her once more. "We'll work it out," he said. "I promise you, no matter what, I'll find a way to deal with your situation."

"Clara is hungry, Daddy," Grace said, entering the room again.

"I have to organize my other daughter, Clara," he said. "What experience do you have with children?" he asked over his shoulder, indicating she should follow him.

"None," she answered softly.

"What of housekeeping?"

She swallowed hard. This wasn't going well. "None of that either."

He turned back to look at her. "What do you have experience with?" He frowned, looking as worried about the situation as she felt.

"None at all. I've not had a job of any sort, or done anything to earn my keep." She chewed on her bottom lip waiting for his response.

"Good. That way I can teach you." He laughed, but she wasn't sure what was so funny.

She must have looked confused because he frowned. "It was a joke really. I have no idea what I'm doing either. Only today my daughter's hair fell out of the braid I'd done, and her pinafore was inside out."

He chucked Grace under the chin. "And I took her out in public like that."

Rose grinned. She couldn't help herself. It was funny in a strange sort of way. "Does that mean I have the job," she asked quietly.

"I think so. If you can stay with the children for a short time, I will make some arrangements." He picked the baby up from the crib. "I shouldn't be gone long."

He changed the saturated diaper, then carried her into the kitchen. "Here," he said, passing the baby over. "I need to warm her bottle."

Rose had no choice – Clara was foisted into her arms. She looked down in alarm at the angelic face. She'd never held a child before.

Clara shoved a tiny fist into her mouth, then rested her head on Rose's shoulder.

Preacher Matthew glanced across at her. "She likes you," he said. "She rarely does that with anyone but me." He winked at her, but she wasn't so confident.

They moved into the sitting room and once she was seated, handed her the baby's bottle. "I'll leave you to it," he said, then was gone.

Little Clara opened her mouth waiting for her bottle, and Rose gently shoved the teat in her tiny mouth. Would she be able to learn how to do all the things the preacher needed? The children needed?

She wasn't sure, but if she wanted to stay here, she would have no choice. She watched the tiny eyes that were watching her. What had these children been through, to have lost their mother at such a young age?

And what of the preacher? He must have endured a lot too. Her heart broke for them all. It was at that moment she knew in her heart she must stay.

Stay for not only herself, but for this family who were desperate for her help.

She looked down into the face of the baby again. Her eyes were trained on Rose, and her little fingers wrapped around one of Rose's. Her heart skipped a beat.

"She likes you," Grace said gently. "I like you too."

A sob was bubbling up in her throat, but she couldn't allow it. Grace got up on her toes and kissed Rose on the cheek.

Clara began to wail. "Put her on your shoulder," Grace instructed. "It's what Papa does." She reached for a towel. "This goes on your shoulder, otherwise she sicks up all over you."

Rose didn't know whether to laugh or be horrified, but added the towel as instructed. It wasn't long before Clara burped then wanted her bottle again.

When it was finished, she was burped again, then fell asleep in Rose's arms while Grace sat at her feet playing with her toys.

She could get very used to this.

Chapter Four

Matthew stood in the doorway watching the scene playing out in front of him.

Grace sat on the floor at Rose's feet, and Clara was tucked safely in her arms. It reminded him of another time – only in that case, it was his dear Alice holding Clara. Emotion hitched in his throat.

He was reluctant to interrupt, but felt the light touch on his arm. Was she thinking the same thing? Staring down at her, he nodded.

"Rose," he said, and her head shot up. "This is Nellie Armstrong. She's going to put you up in her spare room."

He waved the older woman into the room.

Rose studied her, pulling Clara closer to her. "Thank you Mrs Armstrong," she said, seeming a little uncertain. "She had her bottle, then fell asleep," she told Matthew. "I didn't want to disturb her."

He reached out and took the baby. "She never wakes when I put her down, but you weren't to know that." He left the room and placed Clara in her crib.

Matthew couldn't get that scene out of his head. Clara was like a little cherub, and Grace was more than comfortable in Rose's presence.

As he strode back down the hallway, he shook himself. He would not tarnish Alice's memory by having these thoughts. It wasn't right.

Rose and Mrs Armstrong were having a nice little chat, and Grace was snuggled in under Rose's arm. It was obvious the two had hit it off.

He hoped the sleeping arrangements worked out as well.

The older woman turned to him. "I can put Miss Charleston up each night, if you can walk her over before it gets dark?"

"Of course. I'm very grateful to you, Mrs Armstrong, as I'm sure Rose is."

Rose looked from one to the other of them. "Thank you both," she said quietly. "But I have no money to pay for board."

"Rose," Matthew said gently. "It's taken care of. If you look after the children and help with the housework, I'm happy to pay for board and lodgings."

She opened her mouth and he could see she was about to object. "Please don't argue. This arrangement will help me immensely."

She nodded, but he could see she still wasn't convinced.

"Well, I'll be off then. I'll see you both later." Mrs Armstrong chucked Grace under the chin. "And you too, Grace." And then she was gone.

Rose slumped back in the chair. "Why are you doing this for me," she asked the preacher quietly. "You don't know me, not even a little."

He studied her. "I know you're in need of assistance, and I know my daughters adore you." Grace ran to him and cuddled his legs. He picked her up. "I'm also in desperate need of your help."

He sat on a chair opposite her. "I can't continue the way things are, Rose. I can't serve my parishioners *and* raise two small children."

She stared at him, but didn't say a word. "To be honest, Rose, you are a Godsend. The Good Lord has answered my prayers." He reached out and took her hand. "I don't know what I would have done if you hadn't happened along."

"And I don't know what I would have done if I hadn't seen that advertisement."

Matthew prayed this arrangement worked out, because if it didn't he'd be back to square one, and

Rose would once again be homeless. He couldn't allow that to happen.

* * *

"You don't pull my hair like Papa does." Grace smiled up at her, and Rose's heart fluttered.

"That's because I know what it feels like when your hair is pulled." She began to braid the child's hair, very happy with the results.

Grace looked at herself in the mirror. "I look really pretty!" she said, more than a little pleased. Once the braiding was done, she turned and hugged Grace. "I'm glad you came here," she said.

"So am I. Now, let's get you some breakfast."

Rose had slept like a log last night. It was the first time in many days she'd slept in a bed. It might not have been as comfortable as her bed back home, but she still appreciated it.

She'd already helped prepare breakfast for the preacher, and made enough oats for Grace as well. Matthew urged her to eat there too, since she'd overslept and hadn't eaten yet either.

He looked much more relaxed today, and she hoped that was in part due to her presence. She needed to retain this position, even if she had no idea what she was doing.

They were almost done with breakfast when Clara began to wail from her crib. Matthew took a large sip of his coffee. "I'll have to change and feed her," he said, getting up from the table.

Rose frowned. "Isn't that what I'm here for?"

"You're right. Let me show you how." She followed him down the hallway and lifted Clara from her crib. She was drenched and Rose thought she would gag, but forced herself to stay composed.

Matthew told her to lay the baby on the towel he'd placed on the floor, then instructed her on how to change the diaper. She watched out the corner of her eye as he stifled a laugh.

"What's so funny?"

He pulled his expression into one more serious. "That diaper will fall off when you pick her up," he said, still trying to refrain from laughing again.

"No it won't." She picked the baby up, and sure enough, the diaper fell to the floor. Rose felt her chin wobbling. This was so hard – she'd never had to do anything like this before. Ever.

"It took me forever to learn how to do this," he said gently. "Lay her down again and we'll start over."

This time the diaper stayed in place, and she felt a sense of accomplishment. "Do you think you can do that again – when I'm not here?"

"I hope so." Rose carried the wailing baby to the kitchen where she was shown how to prepare the bottle and heat it to the correct temperature.

"You're doing well, Rose. I'll be back for luncheon. Perhaps earlier. Are you able to prepare luncheon? Anything you need you can get from the Mercantile and put it on my account."

She nodded but didn't feel confident.

He leaned across and kissed Clara on the forehead and picked Grace up and hugged her tight. "Be good for Rose, alright?"

"Yes, Papa."

He turned to leave, then turned back to face her. "The perambulator is in the back room. Grace can show you."

In a flash he was gone, and Rose was left alone with two small children she barely knew how to care for.

She sat down and began to feed Clara. Looking down into the tiny face, she wondered if she would pass the test. Could she look after these children in the manner they were used to? Or would she be shipped back home before the week was over?

* * *

Rose lay a blanket on the floor, then placed Clara on it. Grace sat next to her.

She couldn't begin to think about luncheon until she knew what supplies were available to her. Luckily for her, she would sometimes slip into the kitchen and watch cook prepare the meals. She'd learned a thing or two, and cook even let her help on the odd occasion.

Although not when Father was around – cook would have lost her job in a heartbeat if he'd known.

She stepped into the pantry. There were a few staple items like sugar and flour, but not much more. There was a bag of potatoes in the corner, as well as onions. The onions did not smell good.

The cooler was empty except for a lump of ham. Rose sniffed it, happy to find it seemed to be alright.

"Right, Grace," she said. "Let's find that perambulator and go to the Mercantile." Grace led the way to the back room.

Changing Clara first, they headed to the Mercantile. She dreaded going back to face Mrs Stapleton, but she had little choice.

"Good morning," Joe said warmly, and her previous reservations fell away.

His wife stepped out from the storeroom, and she wondered what sort of reception she would get. "I see yer still here," she said, not so warmly.

"Bertha!" Joe said quietly, but not so quietly Rose couldn't hear.

"Yes, I am," Rose said calmly. "I'm looking after the children for Preacher Barnabas. He said to get whatever I need and put it on his account."

Joe nodded. "What can I help you with today, Miss Charleston.

"Rose, please. I need milk, butter, and eggs. That's all for today."

Joe collected the items and placed them in a box. "Oh, wait!" Rose wailed. "Do you sell bread?"

"Of course." He added that to the other items, and wrote them onto the account.

"That's all for today, thank you." She went to take the box, then realized it would be rather awkward carry them while trying to maneuver the perambulator too.

Joe watched her carefully. "Let me," he said. "I'll bring them home for you."

Rose was grateful for his offer, but his wife glared at her. She wasn't sure what she'd done to deserve that treatment.

Once they were outside, Joe turned to her. "Don't worry about the missus. She doesn't like strangers," he said. "She'll eventually come round."

He kept in step with the threesome, and made small talk, telling her about the various people who lived in the town.

"I'm staying with Mrs Armstrong," Rose volunteered.

"I know," Joe said. "Obviously you couldn't stay with the preacher. That wouldn't be right." He stared at Rose momentarily, but the message came through very clearly.

This town obviously looked out for their preacher, and a stranger, like her, would be watched. She would keep to herself, do her job, then go back to Mrs Armstrong's at night. That's all she wanted, and what she would do.

The last thing she wanted was to hitch up with anyone. Especially a man with two small children.

Joe carried the box into the kitchen for her. "You have a good day, Miss Rose," he said, tipping his hat.

Rose watched him leave, and considered herself warned.

* * *

"Papa!" Rose turned to see Preacher Matthew hugging Grace. "I missed you today, Papa." She kissed him on the cheek then slid down to the floor.

"Have you had a good day so far," he asked, turning to Rose.

"Yes, we've had fun. I've made sandwiches for luncheon. I hope that's alright."

He nodded. "Sounds good."

"And I bought supplies for supper."

"Papa, Papa," Grace said, tugging on her father's britches. "We're having pancakes for supper," she whispered loudly.

Rose grinned.

"Are we indeed? That sounds rather mouthwatering." He glanced up at Rose and grinned. "Especially considering we've lived on ham and cheese toasted sandwiches for quite a time."

Now she was horrified. "You're kidding, I hope."

His face dropped, and she knew it was true. Until now, she had no idea how very lucky she was. Hot meals three times a day – she had been thoroughly spoiled. Or if she listened to her father, she'd been totally ruined.

Looking back now, she knew he was right. She had no skills to speak of, and had never held a job. But that was his fault, and she took no blame.

She'd practically begged him to let her get employment. Little did she know then he'd had her life planned out a very long time ago.

Everything made sense now.

She was destined to be the wife of the town lawyer and wouldn't be allowed to work. Jonas Hanson wouldn't want a tarnished wife – that's how he would have seen her, she was certain.

"It's been rather difficult," he said quietly. "I have done my best with what's been dished out."

Rose felt terrible. She hadn't meant to make him feel guilty or inadequate. "I'm sorry, Preacher Barnabas," she said. "I feel terrible for making you feel guilty. That wasn't my intention."

"It's alright. Rose." He began to turn away.

"I'm not the best cook, but I'll try to make a nourishing meal for you and Grace each day."

He stared at her. "Then you must join us."

She began to protest, but he waved her protests away. "I'll let Mrs Armstrong know."

Rose turned to make his coffee. "Rose, it's really nice having someone to come home to," he said quietly. It was then she realized he not only needed help with the children, but he was lonely. He was enjoying her company.

And she was enjoying his.

Placing the food in the middle of the table, she also handed him his coffee. "Come on, Grace. Time for your hands to be washed."

The child pulled a face. "You do what Rose tells you," he said, placing a sandwich on his plate. "When you come back, we'll say thanks for our food."

They sat around the table, hands linked. As Preacher Barnabas said grace, Rose said her own prayer of thanks – for bringing her to this family in need.

The preacher squeezed her hand as if he knew what she was doing. She opened her eyes and glanced at him, and he smiled.

He pulled his hand away, and the warmth she'd felt previously slipped away.

Rose felt more at home here than she'd ever felt back in Idaho. Since permanency wasn't promised, she wasn't sure that was such a good thing. What if she gave her heart to these children, only to have it torn apart?

Chapter Five

"It's a lovely day," Rose said as the preacher headed out the door. "I thought I'd take the children for a walk, if that's alright with you."

He grinned. "Of course. Whatever you want." He pulled Grace into a hug, then turned to Rose again. "Might as well take advantage of it now. The closer it gets to Christmas, the colder it will get."

She hadn't thought of that.

"Give it another week or so and it will be snowing."

Overhearing the conversation Grace ran to him, wrapping her arms around his legs and stared up at him. "Can I build a snowman, Papa?"

He laughed. "It's far too early for that," he said, touching his finger to her nose. "There won't be enough snow for another week or two at least."

"Rose," he said, looking suddenly worried. "You will be here for Christmas, won't you?"

He'd taken her unawares. She hadn't really thought that far ahead. "I have no where else to go," she said quietly. "But if you want me to leave…"

Her heart pounded in her chest. Where would she go? It was perfect here, and far enough away from Idaho that no one would find her. Especially Jonas Hanson.

"No!" It was the loudest Rose had ever heard him speak. And the most assertive.

She stepped back, as did Grace. "Papa," the child said pouting. "You scared me." He reached down and lifted her up, hugging her close.

"I'm sorry, Grace. You too, Rose. I didn't mean to frighten anyone. Please Rose, don't go."

Grace slid down from her father's grasp, tears in her eyes. "Don't go away, Rose. I don't want you to go." Her little arms reached up and Rose squatted down to her level. "Please?"

Rose glanced up at the preacher. He looked as devasted as Grace seemed to be. "We need you here."

She'd been here a little under two weeks, but it felt like forever. It was getting rather tedious being walked back to her rented room every night after supper, but Matthew refused to allow her to walk there alone.

Worst of all, it meant taking the children out in the damp evening air. There was no other option since she couldn't stay overnight with the family. That would not only ruin her reputation, but also the preacher's.

She would simply have to endure it if she wanted to stay here in Dalton Springs and look after the children.

"I like you, Rose. I'll be sad if you go." Tears streamed down her little face.

Rose glanced up at the child's father. "Rose isn't going anywhere," he said assertively. "I know it's a difficult situation," he said, speaking directly to her. "But there isn't much choice. Since we're not married, you can't stay here."

Her hands rose to her chest in shock. "Married?" she squeaked.

He shook his head.

Grace laughed. "You sound funny." Then she skipped away.

"I didn't mean it like that," he said quietly, then headed for the front door. "See you at midday."

Rose cleaned up the kitchen, then prepared the children for their outing. Even after the short time she'd cared for them, there was already a place in her heart for Grace and Clara. Also for their father.

They were not her own children, never would be, but it was beginning to feel that way.

She shook herself. How could one become so attached so soon? "Come on, Grace. Let's get ready for our stroll."

Little Grace came running. "Put on your socks and shoes, and we'll prepare Clara."

"What about Papa?" Her little eyes implored Rose, but sadly she couldn't comply.

"Perhaps another time?"

Grace clapped her hands and ran to get the perambulator. Rose was quickly behind her, not wanting the walls to be destroyed.

As they strolled along the edge of the creek, Rose contemplated her new life. No longer was she bored. The children had brought joy into her life. Not to mention the preacher.

When he arrived home at night, it was like a light turned on inside her. She wasn't sure what that meant except that she liked him.

He was a wonderful father, and she couldn't begin to imagine what he'd been through after his wife had died, trying to raise those girls alone.

In the short time she'd been here, she'd seen a distinct difference in him.

He seemed more relaxed now. Grace seemed very happy, and Clara? Well, she mostly slept and drank. She did have some play time – Rose had seen to that.

"Don't go too far ahead, Grace," Rose called as she took off.

The child looked back over her shoulder. "Alright."

Then suddenly she was out of sight. Panic set in. Rose almost ran as she heard a child's scream. She was certain it was her inquisitive charge.

She quickly caught up to find Grace looking down at her bleeding finger. "What happened?"

She kept her voice soft, although the mishap was a result of misbehavior which was unusual for Grace.

"The plant bit me." Tears rolled down her cheeks, and holding back a smile, Rose wiped her tears away with her kerchief.

She glanced up at the offending plant. "Oh, blackberries! They would be nice for supper." The distraction was enough to stop the flow of tears.

Pulling Grace's pinafore up to form a makeshift bowl, they collected just enough blackberries for supper. "Won't Papa get a surprise?"

Her smile faltering, Grace nodded. "He will."

They began to make their way home again, taking their treasure with them. "It's nearly time for Clara's feed anyway," she told the older child. "And no doubt she is wet."

"Or smelly," Grace added, and holding her nose. Rose couldn't help but laugh.

Life was certainly interesting now. And she felt safe – especially when Preacher Matthew Barnabas was around.

* * *

The preacher looked out across the room.

The church was packed today. His congregation was growing, and it pleased him. It had taken a long time to earn the trust of the people of Dalton Springs. A very long time.

Everyone loved Alice too. After all, what was there not to love?

People were still moving around, and he waited. He watched as Grace wriggled about on the front pew, snuggled close to Rose. Clara was asleep in her lap.

The three of them looked very comfortable together – almost like a real family. Rose had become like family.

If it wasn't for the fact she went back to Mrs Armstrong's place every night, people would probably assume they were.

Mrs Green began to play the organ, and quiet settled across the small building. The door suddenly opened and heads turned. He followed their direction, then sighed.

The circuit Bishop had arrived for a visit. Normally he was advised ahead of time, but not this time.

The visitor made his way to the front pew and sat next to Grace, chucking her under the chin. He spoke briefly to Rose and shook her hand. When he turned to face the front, his expression was stern.

Was there a problem?

Matthew hoped not.

"Thank you everyone for coming today. I'd like to welcome Bishop Holloway to our service today." He indicated the Bishop and continued on with his sermon.

"Let us pray."

Everyone bowed their heads in prayer. He heard Rose shush Grace more than once, and it made him smile. Then Clara began to wail, and he looked up to see Rose rush out of the church with the two children.

He'd missed that. Alice often had to run out. More often than not for a messy diaper than anything.

Then it hit him. Those memories had not visited him for quite some time. Since Rose had arrived, happier times had been on his mind. Prior to that, he was far too busy and stressed to even think about them and could only recall the sad times.

They were singing Onward Christian Soldiers when Rose and the children returned to their seats. He glanced across and saw the Bishop still wore that stern look he'd had earlier.

Whatever was bothering him, Matthew had no idea, but he was certain he'd find out soon enough.

"We will finish with the Lord's Prayer."

Matthew walked slowly down the aisle toward the door. Rose and the girls followed him. He stood firmly and greeted everyone as they left, the Bishop included.

"Can we talk later?" he asked quietly.

"Of course, Bishop Holloway. Why don't you have luncheon with us?" He accepted and Matthew indicated to Rose. "The Bishop is having luncheon with us," he said quietly.

"Oooh, lovely!" she said, obviously delighted.

Normally Matthew felt that way, but today he felt nothing but dread.

"You have no plans to marry, then?"

Rose's head shot up at the Bishop's words. "Marry?" It was the second time in a week the suggestion had been flouted around.

"Marry?" Preacher Barnabas echoed her words.

The Bishop scooped more of the hearty beef soup into his mouth. "This is really good, Rose." He reached for another piece of her homemade bread.

She was becoming a good cook, if she did say so herself. She'd even made blackberry and apple pie for dessert.

"Thank you, Bishop," she said sweetly, feeling a little embarrassed at his praise.

"She's a good cook," Preacher Barnabas said, beaming.

He'd certainly enjoyed her cooking, even if it was basic compared to most.

Rose stood and pulled the pie out of the oven, and began to slice it. She had her back to the two men when the Bishop spoke. "Rose," he said. "Can you sit down a moment? I need to talk to you both."

The Bishop wanted to talk to *her*? How strange. But she complied.

"Yes?" she asked, totally confused.

She watched the preacher as he braced himself. Did he know what the Bishop was going to say? "It's all very innocent, Bishop," he said, preempting the other man's words.

Rose's eyes opened wide. Was he suggesting what she thought he was suggesting?

"Rose is staying with Mrs Armstrong. I can assure you it's all above board."

Rose was fuming. She stood and pulled down four bowls from the overhead cupboard. She didn't dare say a word in case she exploded.

She dished up the dessert and placed a bowl in front of each of the men, and a smaller serve was given to Grace. "Be careful, Grace," she said quietly. "It is very hot."

She placed a bowl of clotted cream in the middle of the table, dishing out a portion to Grace who needed the assistance.

Then she turned away again, preparing coffee for the men.

"Rose, please sit down. I didn't mean to upset you. Either of you." The Bishop dished some cream onto his pie and took a mouthful. "This is really good."

"We picked the blackberries near the creek," Grace said. "See – the plant bit my finger!" She held out her little hand for the men to see her almost indistinguishable cut.

Bishop Holloway reached out and pretended to be concerned. "Goodness me," he said. "Such a sacrifice you made."

Then he eye-balled Matthew, and glanced her way as well.

"Speaking of sacrifices…" He took another mouthful.

"But we haven't done anything," Rose said, wholly shattered at his inference. "I come in daily to look after the children, and go home after supper."

He looked at her gently. "You spend far too much time here," he said calmly. "People are beginning to talk."

"What?" Rose was shocked. They'd done everything possible to sustain her reputation and that of the preacher. She blinked back the tears that were trying to force their way through. "Then I must leave," she said softly.

Grace began to sob. "No, you can't leave me. I want you to stay."

Using great restraint Rose ignored the words. Instead she busied herself with cleaning up the luncheon dishes, not daring to look at either Matthew or the Bishop, lest she begin to sob herself.

She'd begun to see this lovely little town as her home, these people as her family. Even Mrs Stapleton had softened to her.

"Is there no other way," she heard the preacher ask.

She heard a chair push along the floor. "There is no other option," Bishop Holloway said. "Unless Rose leaves. And it's obvious no one here wants that."

Another chair scraped along the floor. "Thank you for a lovely luncheon, Rose," he said. "Shall we meet in the church in say, half an hour?"

And then he was gone.

She had come here to escape one marriage of convenience, and now she was being forced into another. Rose swallowed hard.

What was she going to do?

Chapter Six

Rose faced the preacher. "What just happened?"

Her words faltered, as she knew they would.

He stood stiffly and stared at her. "Honestly? I don't know. I had no indication this was coming."

He glanced down at his still sobbing daughter, then walked over to her and hugged her tight. "It will be alright, sweetheart. Rose isn't going anywhere." He glanced up at her. "Are you?"

Her heart tightened in her chest and she could barely breathe. She had to make a choice – leave this little town and her newly adopted family immediately, or marry the preacher.

She looked from one to the other of them, then squeezed her eyes tightly shut, not allowing the tears to escape. Turning her back on them, she pretended to tidy up from the meal, despite having already done it.

"Rose?" His voice was low and gentle. "I will not force you to do this, but you need to make a decision. Bishop Holloway will be waiting. If you decide against it…"

She hurriedly intercepted his words. "I'll do it." What other choice did she have?

Her words came out much quicker than she'd intended. She had no money, and no where to go. If she stopped looking after the children, there was no reason to stay here, and no means to pay rent to Mrs Armstrong.

It was all a huge mess.

He stood frozen. "You're certain?" He looked as bewildered as she felt. She had no idea what caused this sudden turn of events, and was certain he was in the same situation.

Obviously someone had contacted the Bishop. Was it Mrs Stapleton? Rose wouldn't put it past her, but she had no evidence that was the case.

"Grace, why don't you go and play in the sitting room for a bit?"

It was obvious Grace didn't want to leave, but wanted to see how it all panned out. She couldn't possibly understand what was unfolding, but the emotions were blatantly clear. That much was certain.

When they were alone, Matthew approached her. "You don't have to do this. I'm not going to make you." His hands were on her arms. It was the first time he'd ever touched her, and it felt nice.

His eyes suddenly fell on his hands and he snatched them away.

"Where would I go?" she asked softly. "I have no choice. It wouldn't be so bad, would it? Being married to me?"

He was probably wondering the same thing, but didn't hesitate. "No. It certainly wouldn't. And not much would change – you would sleep here instead of at Mrs Armstrong's. That's it really."

He smiled at her, but she could tell it was a forced smile. "A preacher's wife has certain obligations in the community. Do you think you could manage that as well as the children?"

"What obligations?" It was the first she knew of it.

"Helping with the Ladies Auxiliary. Preparing food for those in need. That sort of thing."

She nodded slowly. Rose had been pushed into a corner. There was little choice available to her, but at least this time she knew what she was getting in to and had a choice. "Whatever it takes. My choices are few."

"It will be a marriage of convenience, of course."

She didn't answer but stared at him. She guessed it would be, he wouldn't be interested in someone like her. "I'll prepare Clara, and tidy myself up. Then we can go." She started to walk away.

"Rose." She turned to face him. "Thank you. I know this is a huge sacrifice for you."

He reached out and took her hand in both of his. Her skin tingled.

She'd seen him do this same thing with his parishioners, so it meant nothing to him. For some strange reason, it meant everything to her.

* * *

They walked into the church together. His church, but right now it felt like he was walking into a building that was unfamiliar.

It was the strangest feeling.

Bishop Holloway sat on the front pew, bible in his hand, head bent. He stood when he saw them enter. "Ah, good." He seemed quite pleased with himself.

"What about witnesses?" It wasn't something Matthew had thought of before.

The Bishop opened the vestry door. "I have them on standby." Mrs Green and Mrs Armstrong entered the church, not meeting his eyes. Would it always be like this from now on? Would these two women who had always been big supporters, shy away in future? He hoped not.

Rose settled Grace onto the front pew, and placed Clara in the perambulator beside her. "You sit quietly," she said softly, handing Grace a book, then kissed her on the cheek. "It won't take long."

Grace did as she was told, but like everyone else, appeared quite bewildered.

The ceremony didn't take long, as he knew it wouldn't. He felt bad for Rose – she'd never been married before and deserved a big wedding. When it was foisted upon you like this had been, there was no time for any sort of preparations.

When it had come time for the part where the Bishop should say *you may kiss the bride*, he omitted that part. Not really surprising given the circumstances.

"Congratulations," Mrs Armstrong said, not sounding very exuberant. She was probably peeved about losing rent. Matthew made a note to give her a bonus for her trouble.

Mrs Green came up to him and gently hugged him, then Rose. She'd always been a hugger, so he wasn't in the least surprise. "What a lovely outcome," she said beaming.

It made him wonder if she realized it was a forced marriage. No matter – it was better if neither woman understood. Word would spread around town quickly, and then people would wonder if Rose was with child.

He groaned inwardly. People could be cruel.

He watched as Rose wandered over to Grace and hugged her tight. "You're a good girl," she told Grace, then kissed her cheek and hugged her. She held her for the longest time, and he wondered if the enormity of what she'd just done had suddenly hit her.

It was after all, a big undertaking. Not only had she become an instant mother, she'd taken on an entire parish.

Although he'd been forced into this situation, he wasn't unhappy about it. Rose was a wonderful person and made a pleasing addition to his family.

"I'm sorry it came to this," the Bishop told him. "But it was taken out of my hands. After the complaint came in…"

"Complaint? Who would…?" It took only a moment to process the answer. "Never mind, I think I know." That nosey Mrs Stapleton – it had to be her. She was always *looking out* for him, according to her. But there was a difference between caring about his welfare and interfering. She'd over-stepped the line this time.

"She was only looking out for you. And Rose," the Bishop said gently.

He shook his head. What did the woman think she would achieve in all of this? To force Rose out of the village? Or to force them to marry?

If it was the latter, she got her way.

According to what Rose had said, Mrs Stapleton hadn't been the most welcoming to her. Hopefully that was all in the past.

From this moment on, life would be different – for both of them. He needed to get home and sort out their new living arrangements. Had Rose realized there were no spare beds? She probably hadn't thought about it. Until this point, there was no need for her to worry.

The more he thought about it, the more he believed it would be upsetting to her.

Time to face the music. He hooked his arm through his wife's and escorted her and the children from the church, and headed next door to their home.

His head was spinning with various thoughts, not all of them goodly.

He stopped at the front door and unlocked it, then scooped Rose up in his arms and carried her across the threshold. Her arms snaked around his neck and she stared into his eyes.

He liked the feel of her arms there, but knew he shouldn't get used to it. Theirs was a marriage of convenience and nothing more.

That's what they'd both agreed to, and he couldn't see Rose changing her mind any time soon.

"What are you doing, Papa?" Grace's voice cut though his thoughts. Just as well too, they were not very gentlemanly.

Still holding Rose, he turned toward his little daughter. "Rose and I got married, Grace. She is your new Mama."

Grace squealed. "I have a Mama?" Tears of happiness streamed down her tiny face and she swiped at them. "Can I call her Mama now?"

She was dancing and crying at the same time. It made his heart swell. He looked at Rose who nodded. "Yes, you can."

He put her down inside the door and Grace ran to Rose. "Mama," she said. "Mama, Mama, Mama!" Her little face was red and blotchy, but it was apparent she was beside herself with joy.

"Your Mama will live with us, Grace. She won't go away again."

"Never?"

"Never."

Grace began to sob and her tears flowed once more.

Matthew had no idea their marriage would affect her in this way. Or that not having a Mama had meant so much to her.

Rose squatted down and opened her arms. Grace ran into them and hugged her as though there was no tomorrow. She held on for dear life, and Rose stood, bringing the overwhelmed child up with her.

She indicated for Matthew to join them and he did. He'd never had a group hug before, but it was amazing. Electricity zinged through him, and he didn't want it to end.

Clara suddenly began to wail, and Rose put Grace's arms around his and lifted the baby up, bringing her into their family circle too.

Today became one of the best in his recollection. This moment was a memory he would not easily forget.

Chapter Seven

It had been a difficult day, to say the least.

The children were now sound asleep in bed, and it was the first time Rose had sat down for any length of time. Between bathing and feeding the two girls, and putting them to bed, she was now exhausted.

There had been no time for talking with Matthew, and indeed, if there had been, the conversation would not have been private.

Personal conversation seemed to be a thing of the past.

"Tired?" Matthew pushed the unburned wood to one side, and scooped up the ashes. She'd never seen him do it before; probably because she'd never been here this late at night.

He turned and tipped the ashes into a metal bucket kept by the fireside.

She yawned at his words and stretched herself out. "I am a little." She watched as the muscles across his back rolled along his body, and quickly averted her eyes. "It seems rather strange being here this late."

He looked over his shoulder at her. "It does. But I'm glad you're here. I hated having to send you away each night."

It was the first time he'd made such an admission and Rose wondered if she should read anything in it.

He stood and dusted his hands of the ash, then reached for the lantern. "Shall we?"

It was the first time Rose had given the sleeping arrangements a thought. As they stepped out of the sitting room, she realized there was no spare bed. Perhaps she could bunk in with Grace?

His hand crept up her back as they headed toward the master bedroom at the back of the house. It felt nice, and a shiver went down her spine.

"Where am I to sleep?" she asked quietly, glancing at him. The lantern sent all sorts of shadows dancing across his face.

She watched as he swallowed then licked his lips. "About that, Rose," he said softly. "You'll have to sleep with me."

Her steps faltered. "With you?" The words came out almost as a squeak, as she tended to do when nervous.

"It's alright, Rose. We *are* married." He held her a little tighter and continued down the hall. "I promise not to touch you…like that." He averted his eyes, as though it was something he didn't want to talk about.

She didn't want to either, but was glad he'd clarified the situation. It was after all, a marriage of convenience.

Mrs Armstrong had retrieved her carpetbag and it sat keenly on the bed, reminding Rose exactly where she was, and what she was doing here.

She opened it and retrieved her night gown. It was made from the best cotton money could buy – of course. Father wouldn't allow anything less. The material was soft and white, and was hand embroidered around the collar. She pulled it up to her cheek and rubbed the soft garment across her skin.

It was an indulgence, she knew, but it wasn't like she'd gone out and bought it since she'd arrived. This had been one of her favorites, which is how it ended up being packed to begin with.

She pulled out her hairbrush and the rest of her meagre belongings. If Mother and Father could see her now, they'd have conniptions. The Preacher's house was smaller than their guest house. But to Rose it had become her home.

"Hang your belongings in the wardrobe." Matthew opened the door, and she noticed the empty space.

It had obviously been his former wife's side of the wardrobe. And now it was hers.

At least her clothes weren't still hanging there.

"I gave all her belongings to those in need, Rose. You needn't concern yourself." Her head shot up. He had an uncanny knack of knowing what she was thinking.

"I, I don't have much. I had to leave most of it behind."

"What happened to you, Rose," he asked. He'd never broached the subject before. Perhaps thinking it was none of his business. But now things were different.

She stayed silent and he held her hand. "Perhaps one day you'll trust me enough."

He suddenly let go of her hand, and took one of the gowns from her, hanging it up for her. Reaching for another one, their hands brushed, and they both stopped, staring into each other's eyes.

His hand curled around hers, then suddenly he let go as though he'd been burned, and turned away.

"I can do it," she said. "You must be tired."

He nodded then left the room, and she heard him enter the bathroom, so took the opportunity to change while he wasn't there.

She felt awkward, as if she didn't belong here, although she knew she shouldn't. She'd had the run of this house for some weeks now, and knew it like the back of her hand.

Except this room.

She'd never ventured in here since it was Matthew's room, and she had no right to be there.

She felt that way now too.

Gingerly, she reached down and turned back the eiderdown. Her hands explored the mattress. It felt nice. Not too hard and not too soft. Rose hoped she could sleep in this strange bed. She'd only just gotten used to the bed at Mrs Armstrong's house.

She sat on the edge, and it felt comfortable.

Matthew strolled in and glanced at her. "Alright?" He didn't wait for an answer but went to the other side of the bed and sat down. He began his evening prayers.

Rose quietly made her way to the bathroom and prepared herself for the night's sleep. She stared at her reflection in the mirror and wondered how she'd ended up here. At the preacher's house, as the preacher's wife.

It was greed, as it always was.

Jonas Hanson had obviously offered her father a big ransom for his young daughter. Worse still, her father had accepted. The thought was enough to make Rose feel ill.

She reached up and pulled the pins out of her hair, then brushed it out. She couldn't help but yawn, and made her way back to the master bedroom.

Thankfully Matthew was sound asleep. She had a reprieve. For tonight at least.

* * *

Her eyes fluttered open, and Rose knew it was early morning. Likely around dawn. As she tried to climb out of bed, a large hand gripped her around the waist, and it was all she could do to stop from screaming.

She slowly turned in the bed and saw Matthew laying there, his eyes closed, his face relaxed. She'd almost forgotten the activities of the day before.

How that was possible, she would never know.

She'd always seen him as her employer, and not really thought of him as a man. Now that Matthew was her lawfully married husband, that was beginning to change.

She stared into his face. He was handsome in his own way. She didn't know exactly how old he was, but figured he must be at least thirty. Maybe more. One of these days she'd ask him.

His slightly too long brown hair was ruffled from the night's sleep. It made her smile. He was always so perfect – perfectly dressed, perfectly polite, perfectly everything. This was the first time she'd seen anything out of place on him.

She liked it.

His mouth opened slightly and she noticed for the first time his lips. His mouth was the perfect size for his oval-shaped face. And right now she wanted to lean in and kiss those perfect lips, but she couldn't bring herself to do it.

Not only would it wake him up, but he'd think her a hussy. And that just wouldn't do.

"Mama! Papa!" Grace ran into the room and jumped on the bed between them. She wore a huge grin.

Matthew's eyes opened in fright.

"Really, Grace?" Rose asked her quietly. "You woke your Papa." Grace's chin quivered, and she pulled her new daughter into an embrace. "You must be more gentle next time."

"Good morning." He continued to lay on the pillow, and looked very happy with himself. Like the cat who stole the last of the cream.

As if on cue, Clara began to wail. "When will she stop doing that?" Grace asked, exasperated.

"Very soon. It's time Clara was eating some regular foods." Matthew raised his eyebrows in question. "I've been reading up on it. She needs to be weaned off the bottle full-time and have some solids introduced."

He slid out from underneath the blankets and headed for his clothes. It felt strange seeing her employer in a nightgown. Only he wasn't her employer anymore. He was her husband.

Rose had to constantly remind herself of that fact. It seemed like a dream, but it was indeed true.

She pulled back from Grace and forced herself out of the warm bed. It had been very comfortable, and for that she was very grateful.

Grace jumped down, and Rose made the bed with the child's help. "This will be our special job every day, Grace."

You'd have thought she'd told her daughter she was taking her to the circus, she was so joyful. If nothing else, she'd learned over the past weeks it didn't take much to make this little girl happy. She'd endured so much sadness in her short life, and Rose was overjoyed to be part of the reason for the change in her.

She knew a lot had changed over the past weeks, not only for her, but for Grace who needed a mother-figure in her life. Now, thanks to Mrs Stapleton, she had not only a mother-figure, but a mother.

She took the girl by the hand and led Grace to her room. "Since Clara has stopped bellowing for now, let us find you some clothes. Can you dress yourself?"

"Yes. I'm a big girl." Grace grinned at her, but Rose had her doubts. Regardless, she pulled some clothes out of the cupboard and laid them on the bed.

"Of course you are. Get dressed while I see to Clara, then we'll get breakfast." As if the timing was perfect, Clara began to wail again, and Rose headed to her room.

"Oh dear, Clara," Rose said, almost gagging at the smell. "Let's get you out of that soiled diaper and cleaned up, then we'll get you fed."

She filled the bowl from the jug, and gave Clara a quick wash. "You must feel better now." Lifting the baby, she rested Clara against her shoulder and headed for the kitchen where she found her husband.

"Can you take her while I dress?" She passed Clara over. "That book I've been reading says she should be sitting up by now."

"Should we be worried?" He looked very concerned. "Perhaps the doctor should check her over."

Rose filled the kettle with water, before leaving the room. "Let's try and help her to sit up first, then if it doesn't work, we can take her to be checked."

She came back a short time later, and Clara followed her every move. It wasn't lost on Rose.

She was the one who'd been feeding and changing her most of the time, and so she'd become Clara's carer in the child's mind. It was only natural she'd come to see Rose this way.

She handed Matthew a warm bottle of milk. "If you can feed her, I'll make breakfast." He complied and she set about doing what she'd intended all along, only without the audience.

"Scrambled eggs with bacon this morning. And toast."

She set about her tasks. By the time the bottle of milk was empty, the food was ready. "We'll need to get a high chair for her soon. Once she's sitting up, Clara can join us at the table."

"There should be one in the store-room from when Grace was a baby."

"I didn't see one there." Rose set her husband's food in front of him, and took the baby.

"It's covered with a sheet. I'll pull it out later." He got stuck into his breakfast. "This is delicious," he said between mouthfuls.

Rose placed Clara back in her crib where she knew she'd sleep for a while.

She'd learned a lot from that book, and now that she'd taken on the role of mother to the two girls, would begin to wean the baby out of her many sleeps.

"Is there anything I need to do today – as the preacher's wife, I mean?" Rose asked quietly as she ate her own breakfast.

Matthew glanced up from his coffee. "Don't stress over it. You'll have time to settle in – a week at least I should think. The Ladies Auxiliary will contact you when they're ready. They'll be pleased to have your assistance."

He drank down the last mouthful, then pushed his chair back. "I'll light the fire in the sitting room, and then I'll be on my way."

He hugged Grace, then walked over to Rose. He gently held her arms, then leaned in to kiss her. The closer he got, the more she anticipated his kiss. His lips were an angel's breath away from her mouth when he glanced up at her, then suddenly changed tack and gently kissed her on the cheek.

He quickly left the room without a word.

Her face tingled, but Rose was disappointed. As his wife, she'd expected him to kiss her more intimately. It was his right to do so, and she couldn't figure out why he didn't.

"Why did Papa kiss you?" Grace asked, her curiosity getting the better of her.

"Because Papa and I got married yesterday. I'm your Mama now, remember?" Grace nodded so she continued. "So now Papa is allowed to kiss me, and hug me, just like he does to you and Clara."

"Oh. Alright." And then she continued eating, her curiosity satisfied.

Matthew put his head around the door. "I'm off now. The fire is roaring."

"Thank you."

"You can kiss Mama now," Grace said, then filled her mouth again.

Rose and Matthew stared at each other, then began to laugh.

Her life had changed dramatically, but Rose wouldn't have it any other way. For the first time she could remember, she was happy. Truly happy.

And she knew she was making a difference. If not to Matthew, certainly to the two girls who now had a Mama.

Chapter Eight

It was chilly outside, and Rose dressed the girls in their warm coats and gloves, then headed out for a quick stroll.

The creek had become Grace's favorite place to visit, especially when she was able to pick blackberries, so they spent a little time there. Rose watched her like a hawk, ensuring she didn't go close to the water.

They visited the Mercantile on the way home to pick up a few small necessities. Believing Mrs Stapleton to be the cause of their forced marriage, Rose was reluctant to go inside, but she would have to do it sometime. She slowly opened the door, and saw Joe was stacking shelves, so pushed the door wider.

"Hello Mr Stapleton," Grace said, skipping toward the store-owner.

"Hello little one," he said cheerfully, then turned toward Rose.

"Good morning, Miss Charleston."

Her head shot up. Perhaps he was genuinely unaware of her change in marital status. "It's Mrs

Barnabas now, but like I've said before, call me Rose."

His eyes opened wide, and he stood staring until he realized what he was doing. He scratched his head, then tugged on his apron, apparently not knowing what else to do. "When did this happen?"

"Yesterday." She wasn't going to volunteer anymore information than was absolutely necessary. And she certainly wasn't going to accuse his wife of over-stepping the mark, as she surely had. Rose was almost positive of it.

"I have a Mama now," Grace offered, a huge grin on her little face.

Joe leaned down to her level. "That's wonderful," he said, then straightened up again. "What can I do for you, Rose?"

She gave him her small list, and waited while he collected them up for her. She was making Apple and Cinnamon Muffins this morning. She knew Matthew would enjoy them, and so would Grace. They were having hearty vegetable soup for luncheon, and it was already on the stove cooking.

Rose was enjoying her new life in Dalton Springs, particularly her new role as a mother.

"Here you are, Rose." Joe handed the items over, as well as a small wrapped package.

She looked it over, not recognizing the item. "What's this, Joe? It's not something I asked for." She brought it up to her nose – the aroma was delightful.

He grinned. "It's a small gift. For your wedding. From the missus and me."

"Oh! Thank you, Joe. That's so very kind of you." She opened the packaging to discover a cake of perfumed soap. Rose's heart soared. What a lovely thing to do.

Mrs Stapleton put her head around the door. She scowled when she saw Rose standing there. "Congratulations are in order," Joe told his wife. "Rose and the preacher got hitched."

Rose watched as a smirk appeared on the older woman's face, then quickly disappeared. She was right – it was Mrs Stapleton! What a nasty thing to do. But Rose, being the good Christian woman she was, didn't retaliate.

"Congratulations Mrs Barnabas." There was no suggestion of joy in her voice, but Rose detected a hint of arrogance.

"Thank you for the gift," she said, all sweetness in her voice.

Bertha's eyes opened wide, then she stormed out of the room. Rose felt a tad guilty for riling the woman up, but there was also an element of satisfaction.

"Thanks again, Joe. Now we need to hightail it home and get baking."

She headed out the door and was about to cross the main road when Grace squealed. "Mama! Mama! It's snowing," she said, holding her hand out to catch the few flurries that tumbled from the sky.

"So it is," Rose said, trying to sound as excited as the small child beside her.

"We can build a snowman now." Her little face looked up at Rose expectantly.

She squatted down to her daughter's height. "There's not enough snow yet, sweetheart. Perhaps in a few days." Grace pouted, but accepted what she'd been told.

As they arrived home, Rose felt as though someone was watching them. She quickly turned but there was no one there. She must have been imagining it.

She looked down into the perambulator to see little Clara trying to push herself up. Excitement filled her. Was she now ready to sit up?

Rose would ensure she was encouraged in this area.

She unlocked the door and entered. Thanks to Matthew lighting the fire this morning, the cottage was warm.

They moved into the sitting room and she added more logs on the fire, then returned the guard to stop Grace getting too close.

After changing and feeding Clara, they moved into the kitchen, where Rose began baking. Grace was enthralled watching her, and was invited to help. She snatched up the opportunity.

"Tip the flour into the bowl," Rose instructed, having already measured the ingredients. She handed Grace a spoon and let her stir the flour. "Now add the sugar and stir it all up."

Grace was in her element. Had she never cooked before? It was highly unlikely since her mother had died when she was just a tot.

Leaning into the cinnamon, Grace suddenly pulled back. "That stuff tickles my nose!" They both laughed. Rose added the eggs and milk, then the chopped apples, and let her daughter stir it all up with a little help.

Before long the muffins had been placed in the oven and would soon be ready. Rose groaned as she glanced across at the table. "What a mess," she whispered so Grace wouldn't hear. It wasn't her fault – she was just a child.

It was gratifying she'd enjoyed herself, and it surely helped the two connect as mother and daughter.

"What's all this?" Matthew laughed as he entered the room.

"We made muffins, Papa! It was fun!" He walked over and gave his daughter a hug, then moved to Rose and looked into her face.

His hand came up and brushed against her cheek. "You have flour on your face," he said quietly as he stared longingly into her eyes.

She licked her lips, and he moved closer. Rose was certain he wouldn't kiss her with Grace in the room, and began to move away. He held her shoulders and brushed her lips gently, then stared into her eyes.

A zing ran through her body at the contact, and it shocked her to her core. If a light touch like that could make her feel this way, how would she feel when they really connected?

Rose felt the heat rise up her face, and turned away. But not before she saw Matthew grinning. How rude!

She quickly cleared the mess from the table, then cleaned Grace up, ready for luncheon.

"It's hearty soup again today," she told her husband, then pulled two bowls out of the cupboard. "Yours has been cooling for awhile, Grace. Let me check if it's cool enough." She grabbed a teaspoon and checked the temperature. "Perfect."

Matthew watched her every move, but it didn't make her feel uncomfortable. Well, perhaps a little. He'd never done it before, but they weren't married before. Should that even make a difference?

She shrugged her shoulders, then dished out soup for Matthew and herself. After placing his meal in front of him, she poured the coffee.

The moment she sat down they joined hands and said thanks for their food.

"Have you had a good day so far," she asked when the prayer was ended.

Matthew glanced at her. "Excellent. Rose, I haven't said it before, but having you here has made a huge difference. Now that we're married…"

"Nothing has changed much," she interrupted. "The only difference is I no longer have to leave at night."

Realizing the implications of her words, her face heated up. He chuckled but didn't say anything. Besides, she'd already said enough.

"We went to the creek, Papa," Grace said, interrupting the awkward silence that had come over the room.

He rubbed his hands together. "Does that mean we get to have blackberry pie tonight," he asked her conspiratorially.

She turned toward Rose. "Does it, Mama?"

Rose glanced from Grace to Matthew. "Perhaps." She turned to the small child looking innocently at her. "Soon we won't be able to go to the creek, Grace. The snow will make it too cold."

Grace pouted. "But I like going there."

"Mama is right," Matthew said sternly. "There will be other times." He pointed at her food, and Grace began to eat again.

She was such a well-behaved child, and Rose was thankful for that. She was a sweetie too, but had been dealt a very difficult hand in life.

Rose was very grateful she'd been able to alleviate some of the stress that had held this family at bay for such a long time.

Matthew was much more relaxed now than when she arrived, and the children seemed less stressed too.

"Oh!" Rose suddenly jumped up from the table, remembering the muffins.

"They smell delicious," Matthew said, breathing in the fragrant aroma. "They look good too."

Placing them on a cooler, Rose put them aside, and returned to the table.

"It's nice having you home for luncheon," she told her husband. "My father never once came home in the middle of the day."

He swallowed down the last of the soup before answering. "I'm lucky that most of my work is close by, but there will be times I have to travel to outlying areas. I may even be gone overnight on occasion. I haven't been able to do that since…" He stopped in his tracks, not wanting to utter the words that might upset his little daughter.

"I understand. You do what you have to do, and I'll cope here." She didn't like the thought of being alone in the cottage with only the girls, but there was no chance Rose would hamper her husband's progress. The word of God must be heard, and she wouldn't stand in the way.

Bringing the muffins to the table, Matthew reached for one. "You are a breath of fresh air in my life, Rose," he said, glancing across at her.

"Thank you," she said meekly. Warmth spread through her at his words. Winning his confidence and his praise made her feel good.

He finished his coffee then stood to leave. "You're not having a second muffin?" She smiled at him and he sat down again.

"If you insist," he said, grinning.

Rose enjoyed living here. Being here with Matthew and the children. Her parents home was never like this. She'd always felt alone and lonely. Her days were filled with boredom, and she certainly hadn't felt loved.

Coming to Dalton Springs had changed her entire life – for the better.

If only she had a real marriage, and not one of convenience.

She'd been a convenience to her parents, especially her father who had bargained to get rid of her. She didn't want to be a convenience to her husband, who was obviously a loving and caring man.

She sighed. If only things could change.

Chapter Nine

"I missed you today."

Matthew reached across the bed and pulled Rose toward him. He'd spent the best part of the day visiting parishioners in outlying areas; people he had been unable to visit for some months.

He'd become so used to coming home at midday and spending time with his family, that he really missed it when he hadn't been able to do so.

Despite that, it was a good day. Mrs Corcoran had broken her leg a week earlier, and this was the first time Matthew had the opportunity to catch up and ensure she was coping.

Her sister had moved in temporarily, so all was well.

Mr Blackstone, who lived about four miles further on was heartbroken. His wife had died in childbirth and he was reluctantly contemplating re-marrying. He couldn't work the farm while looking after the child, who was still at the stage where a lot of attention was needed.

While Matthew could totally relate, and felt re-marrying had been the best thing in his situation, it didn't mean it would work for this widower.

He would see if the Ladies Auxiliary could perhaps put together a food hamper to help Mr Blackstone out in the immediate future. They might even be able to help with caring for the baby to help relieve his anxiety.

It had worked wonders in his hour of need.

Rose rolled toward him and smiled. In the days since they'd married, they'd seemed to be getting closer. It was never his intention, given they were forced into this situation, but he was growing more and more fond of sweet Rose.

He tightened his grip on her, and she didn't pull away. Her cheeks took on a touch of pink. Was she embarrassed? He hoped not. They were man and wife – there was nothing to be embarrassed about.

He leaned in and lightly kissed her lips. She didn't back away, but stared into his eyes.

"Matthew?" she asked softly. He knew what she meant – she was asking what he was up to. So far all their kisses had been chaste. Sure, they'd been nice, but he wanted more, and he sensed she did too.

His head ducked lower and he gently kissed her neck, his hands sliding up to her shoulders. "Rose," he said quietly. "I have come to have feelings for you." He felt her stiffen under his touch.

Did she not feel the same way?

"And I for you," she said softly. "I'm not sure what that means."

Warmth spread through him. Did that mean they could truly become a married couple? Would she agree to a union that included consummating the marriage, and eventually having children?

The only way he would find out was to ask. "Rose," he said slowly. "What I said before about having feelings for you, was only half true."

She stiffened again. "What I feel for you is more than that." He stared into her mesmerizing blue eyes. "Despite not knowing each other for a terribly long time, I've fallen in love with you, Rose."

"Oh Matthew," she said, joy in her voice. "I fell in love with you soon after we met. But I kept it to myself as I didn't think it was appropriate."

His heart thundered in his chest, and his lips covered hers. Rose didn't pull back or deny his advances.

Soon they were making love, and Matthew hoped and prayed they would one day make a child of their own.

* * *

Clara wailed and Rose began to climb out of bed before Matthew had a chance to look at her.

Last night was not what she'd expected, and today she felt embarrassed. Could she ever look at him again?

"Rose," he whispered. She turned back to face him, against her better judgement, and felt the heat surge up her face.

He leaned in and kissed her lips. "Don't be embarrassed," he said, brushing his fingers across her tinged cheeks. "It's natural, and what all married people do."

She didn't know how to answer that, so didn't. "I have to get Clara up." She left the room, but heard the movement of the bedding behind her as he climbed out.

"Mama." Grace wiped the sleep out of her eyes as she walked down the hallway.

"Good morning, Grace," Rose said, heading toward the wailing child.

Rose had never envisioned her life this way, but was grateful for the way it had turned out. She grimaced when she thought about what might have been had she stayed at her parent's home and married Jonas Hanson.

She was even grateful for the spiteful Mrs Stapleton for her interference. Without her, she wouldn't be married to a man she loved.

As she approached the crib, Clara watched her every move. She reached out and held tight to the bars facing Rose, then pulled herself up to a sitting position.

"Papa, Papa!" Grace yelled, and Matthew came running.

"What's wrong? Is Clara alright?" His stricken expression proved his concern for his children.

Rose grinned at him. "Look at what your daughter is doing."

"Good job, Clara," he said. "And I think you mean our daughter." He pulled Rose close and hugged her tight.

"My goodness, whatever is that smell?" Realization dawned and he backed away. "I'll go and light the fire, and… put on the kettle," he said, making a hasty retreat.

Rose laughed, then got to work with the job at hand. How he had ever managed to care for the girls before she arrived, she had no idea. Or perhaps he'd gotten used to her doing the 'dirty' work.

Either way, he loved those children and would do anything for them. She hoped he felt the same way about her.

"What are you doing today," Rose asked as she entered the kitchen carrying Clara.

The kettle boiled and she handed Clara over to her father while Rose prepared her bottle, as had become the daily routine.

"I'm still catching up on visits to my shut-in parishioners. That part of my duties suffered a lot before you arrived."

She turned to him and frowned. "Most people were delighted to see the children, but some were not. I didn't have a lot of choices then," he explained.

She handed over Clara's warmed up bottle, and began cooking breakfast. Bacon and eggs with toast today. She knew Matthew was enjoying having a cooked breakfast each day because he'd told her so.

He and Grace were eating much better. He'd told her that too. Although she'd been shocked at first, she totally understood. He was a grieving father who had little experience with children, and had no idea how to cook.

They were both looking better since she'd arrived. Learning to cook had been difficult for her too, but after rummaging at the Mercantile, she'd managed to find a beginner's cookbook. It had been a lifesaver – for all of them.

Rose sat as they linked hands and Matthew said a prayer of thanks for their meal, then placed his food in front of him. She took Clara and laid her on the floor on a blanket.

"I'm keeping Clara up longer today," she said. "I think she's sleeping far too much."

Matthew glanced up at her. "You're her mother," he said. "You get to make decisions about her welfare."

"You don't mind?"

He pushed his chair back and stood, stepping toward her. He held her by the shoulders and moved closer. "I trust you with my children's lives, Rose. I've been doing so since you arrived. Why would that change now?"

She hadn't really thought about it before, but he was right. He had put his girl's lives in her hands. She glanced up to see him staring into her eyes.

The longing was unmistakable. He gently kissed her lips, then went back to his breakfast.

She watched as Grace's eyes went from one to the other of them. If it wasn't so sweet it would be funny. But Rose knew this was all new to Grace as well.

The poor girl must be totally confused about the new family dynamic. First Rose arrives to care for Grace and Clara, then suddenly she's their Mama.

Heck, Rose would be confused too.

"I thought we might clean up the vegetable garden a bit more today, Grace. Before it gets too cold for us to do it." They'd done a little each day, and Grace loved that part of their day.

She clapped her little hands. "Can we do it now?"

Rose would love to give in to her whims, but it wasn't possible. "Eat your breakfast first, then we'll see."

She nodded and Matthew grinned at her antics. He drank down the last swallow of his coffee, then hugged his girls – all three of them.

"I'll be off then," he said, then left without another word.

Rose finished off her breakfast, then dressed. It wasn't too bad weather-wise so far today, but they would still need their coats. With Christmas barreling closer, and snow becoming heavier by the day, they would need to rug up.

With Clara propped up with a pillow in the perambulator, they headed for the backyard. Rose stood back and watched Grace pull at the overabundance of weeds.

Rose used a trowel and gently moved the dirt about. It wasn't long before she was able to retrieve six fully grown potatoes.

"Oh Mama," Grace said, watching her with awe. "Can we have them for supper?"

Rose reached down and pulled out a bunch of carrots as well. "We certainly can. These will make a nice stew."

She looked up as snow landed on Grace's face and in Clara's hair. "That's enough for today," she said, opening the door.

Rose was beginning to understand why her father's gardener had told her many times he loved his job. It had brought a lot of satisfaction pottering around in this little vegetable patch, and she would never tire of working it.

She washed the vegetables, then left them to drain. They went into the sitting room, where she sat Clara on the floor, leaning up against the chair Rose sat on, pillows surrounding her.

She was finally ready to sit up, and Rose would help by showing her how. It was another satisfying part of her new role. "Why don't you find some toys for Clara to play with?"

Soon the baby was surrounded by toys, and sat happily playing. Grace sat across from her, encouraging her sister. She looked so pleased with herself, and Rose wondered if Grace had longed for the day her little sister would be able to play with her.

Rose watched the two girls interact and wished she'd had a sister. Then again, her sister would have been placed in the same situation Rose had been – having to run for her life.

There was a knock to the door, and she slowly opened it. They weren't expecting guests. To her surprise, there was no one there, and the gate stood wide open. Rose knew for certain Matthew would not have left the gate ajar.

Who had played this trick on her? She shrugged her shoulders and closed the gate, then went back to her girls. Clara was tiring and beginning to topple sideways.

Rose changed her diaper and put her down for a rest.

Grace was playing happily in the sitting room when she returned, so she sat on the chair and rested for a moment. Staring out the window, she saw the silhouette of a man hidden in the shadows.

She shuddered. Was it the same person who'd knocked on the door?

"Mama! Look at this." Her attention was taken by the toy Grace wanted to show her. When she glanced up again, he was gone.

If he was even there. Perhaps her imagination was playing tricks on her. But Rose knew the open gate was not a figment of her imagination.

Chapter Ten

Two days had passed but Rose couldn't get the incident of the open gate out of her mind.

She hadn't mentioned it to Matthew, afraid it would worry him. Instead she would keep her eyes open whenever they left the house.

If such a thing happened again, she would definitely inform her husband.

He was due home in less than an hour, so they hurried to the Mercantile. Hearty soup was on the stove, biscuits were cooling on the counter. Luncheon was ready.

Until she discovered the butter was almost non-existent. She's been so worried about her unseen visitor, she'd let her household duties fall behind.

The children were well wrapped in their warm coats, gloves and hats, and they headed out. The flurries were getting heavier by the day, much to the delight of Grace. She had her sights set on building a snowman, and was getting impatient at the long wait.

Rose couldn't blame her. She was a small child, and had no concept of time. It would be at least another week before they experienced heavy snowfall, according to Matthew.

Grace raced ahead as they arrived at the Mercantile. She had a special relationship with Joe – he was almost like an uncle.

"Good morning, little one," he said, as she ran toward him.

She grinned shyly at him. "Good morning," she said back. "We need butter."

He looked to Rose. "We do. I didn't realize I was so low."

Joe went out the back to retrieve the butter for them. He quickly returned. "Thanks Joe. You've saved me."

They headed to the door and were about to depart the store, when a familiar figure approached the store. She would recognize him anywhere.

She scurried to the back corner of the store where they couldn't be seen from the front of the store, and Joe stared at her.

Once the door opened, she was sure he'd understand.

"Morning," he told the stranger, in a not so friendly fashion. Not for Joe anyway, Rose decided. "What can I do for you?"

"I'm looking for someone. Rose Charleston." Rose would know that voice anywhere.

Joe went quiet, and Rose held her breath. "Ain't no Rose Charleston here," he answered truthfully.

"Huh. I was told she was here in Dalton Springs."

Rose heard papers shuffling around, then Joe replied. "I know everyone in this town, and there ain't no Rose Charleston."

He wasn't lying. She was now Rose Barnabas.

Joe was a good Christian man who didn't lie, but she also knew he would protect her if it push came to shove.

She heard the door open and the bell tinkle, but was too afraid to come out of hiding. She waited for a couple of minutes, and finally Joe came to her.

"Who is he?" Joe asked sternly.

Rose swallowed. She'd hoped by coming here she had seen the last of Jonas Hanson, but apparently it wasn't to be.

"I, I was being forced to marry him," she said quietly. "So I ran away."

"Well you're married now, so it's too late. He can't have you."

She nodded, not sure how to answer. Since she and Matthew had consummated their marriage, could she still be forced into marriage with Jonas?

He was a lawyer, he would know all the possible ways to make her. She wanted to cry, but had to stay strong for Grace. It would upset the child terribly.

"Wait here." Joe indicated for her to stay put and went out of the store, looking all around, then returned. "I can't see him, so I think he's gone."

She began to push Clara out of the corner, clasping Grace's hand at the same time.

"To be certain, I'm coming with you. I want to make sure you get home safe." Rose opened her mouth to argue, but he stopped her. "I owe the preacher that much, and I don't want to see a sweet thing like you hurt. Or the children."

"Thank you," she said quietly.

"Bertha, look after the store," he bellowed, checking outside again, then led them back to the preacher's cottage.

He didn't ask questions of her, in fact, Joe didn't say a word.

They arrived at the same time as Matthew. Rose thanked him, and he began to walk away when they were joined by an unwelcome guest.

Joe rejoined them, and Matthew gave him a curious look.

Jonas reached out and grabbed Rose by the arm. "You're coming with me," he bellowed, trying to drag her away.

"No I'm not. I'm already married," she yelled, pulling back in vain.

"Get your hands off my wife," Matthew demanded, but Jonas ignored him. Matthew stepped between them, and Joe grabbed the intruder.

Grace began to scream. "Let go of my Mama!" She kicked him on the shin, but Jonas continued on his endeavor.

Tears rolled down Rose's cheeks. Her life had been wonderful, and now this.

"What's going on here?" It was a voice Rose didn't recognize, but she felt relieved when she noticed the sheriff's badge.

"She's my betrothed." Jonas was adamant.

"Rose is my wife," Matthew said determinedly.

Jonas continued his grip on Rose, and tried to drag her away.

Rose could see Matthew getting angrier by the moment, and Joe stretched himself to his already tall height. They were both ready to fight for her.

"Let the lady go." The sheriff spoke low but clearly. When Jonas still refused, the sheriff pulled out his gun.

Rose gasped.

Joe snatched up Grace and pulled Clara out of the way. Matthew stepped toward Rose, knowing his children were safe. The horror on his face was palpable.

"Last chance," the sheriff said firmly, and Jonas finally let go his grip.

He was handcuffed and marched to the jail. Rose was shaking and crying, and Matthew pulled her close, wrapping his arms around her.

She didn't want him to ever let her go.

* * *

With less than a week until Christmas, the snow was finally heavy enough for Grace to make her much-wanted snowman.

He was a little lopsided, and his face was all out of shape, but no one cared. She was having fun, and that was all that mattered.

Despite being rugged up, her little teeth were chattering, but no way was she going back inside.

"I'll tell you what, Grace," Rose said gently. "If you come inside and warm up for a little while, after we eat we can go and watch the Christmas tree being put up."

Her little eyes opened wide. "Really?" she asked excitedly.

It would be a big day for her, but it would also be a day to remember. Since arriving in Dalton Springs, Rose had learned that memories made together as a family were more important than anything else.

"We even have a special decoration to put on the tree," she told the shivering child. "Come inside and we'll get ready."

Since she'd found out it was tradition for newlyweds to add a decoration to the tree, Rose had made it her mission to create one.

Grace ran into the house and headed straight to the sitting room, which was the warmest room in the house. It didn't take long for the chattering to subside.

Clara sat at Rose's feet and played happily as she sat up unaided. She had begun to feed the baby a few solids, and she was more than happy now.

Matthew arrived home for luncheon and stood in the doorway observing the joyful sight. Rose could vividly recall him doing the same thing when she'd first arrived a few months earlier. Only this time he had a look of contentment instead of one of sadness.

"Papa!" Grace ran toward her father and wrapped her little arms around his legs. "We're going to see the Christmas tree soon."

He reached down and pulled her up into his arms. Rose watched as he kissed her forehead and whispered something in her ear. Grace wriggled her way down to the floor and ran off.

"What did you say to her?" Rose asked, perplexed.

"I told her if she had a rest on her bed, there might be a surprise in a few days."

Clara's eyes began to close, and she started to topple sideways. Rose knew it was time for her to rest too.

She picked the baby up and headed toward her room.

When she returned, Matthew was standing in front of the fire, a smile on his face.

"What?" Rose asked, sensing something was up.

His smile became a grin. "Am I not allowed to have my wife all to myself?" He opened his arms and she walked into them.

"I love you more than life itself, Rose," he whispered in her ear.

Rose rested her head on his chest. "I love you too, Matthew. Until I came here, I had no idea what a real family could be like." She lifted her head and glanced up into his face.

"You were a lost soul," he said gently. "But I was lost too - you saved us both."

Tears rolled down her cheeks, and he brushed them away. She'd never thought about it before, but he was right, they were lost, but now they'd found each other.

With Jonas safely tucked away in jail, she no longer had to concern herself with him turning up to claim her.

Perhaps one day she may even have a reconciliation with her parents. Matthew was certainly keen for that to happen.

Only ten minutes had passed before Grace came running out of her room. "I've had a rest, Papa," she said excitedly.

Rose pushed herself out of her husband's arms. She felt so loved and so safe with him. "Time for luncheon, and then we can go and see the Christmas tree," she told the child.

Grace ran into the kitchen and sat at the table. Something she rarely did without instruction.

They said a prayer for their food, then tucked in. Grace ate with more vigor than usual. It made Rose smile.

"I have the rest of the day off," Matthew said, surprising her. "I planned it so we could spend the afternoon together."

Rose did not complain.

With Grace in his arms, and Rose by his side, Matthew looked down at Clara rugged up in the perambulator.

They waited until almost the last minute to arrive, not wanting the children to become agitated at the wait. The younger men of the town had wound a rope around the trunk of the huge tree, and everyone was instructed to move back.

The last thing the Mayor wanted was for someone to be injured.

Matthew looked down at his daughters and his wife. This time last year it was a totally different scenario. He was certain Alice would be looking down on them with a sense of approval.

Rose was a good mother to the girls, and would be no different with their future children. A smile crossed his face.

A few months ago, none of this was even on his mind.

"Papa! Papa!" Grace yelled in his ear, startling him. She grabbed at his chin and faced him toward the tall tree. "Look, Papa! It is a giant tree," she said, still shouting.

His heart was full of love, for this town, for his family, and for Rose, who now had Clara in her arms. The baby's eyes followed every movement as the tree was raised up.

"Can you take Clara," Rose asked, indicating for him to put Grace down. She reached into her pocket and pulled out the decoration he knew she'd been making with Mrs Armstrong's help.

She squatted down to Grace's height and whispered in her ear, then reached for the little girl's hand. Together they walked over to the now secured tree and added their decoration.

Grace turned back to look over her shoulder and glance at her father – a huge grin on her face.

His heart swelled at the scene before him. This Christmas was sure to be filled with joy.

Epilogue

One year later…

As they sat in the sitting room buttoning eighteen-month-old Clara's coat, Grace put on her own coat. With the warmth of the fire and the aroma of Christmas baking, the place felt very homely.

Matthew thought back to a year ago. They were doing something similar this time last year, but this year was very different.

This year they had welcomed their new baby, a son. Joshua Mark Barnabas had been welcomed into the world only two weeks ago. Rose's parents had arrived soon after they'd received word of their first grandchild.

It was a tearful reunion, but one that needed to happen.

Matthew sat back and watched the scene play out before him. This was his family, his reason for living.

"Time to go," Rose said quietly, not wanting to wake Joshua.

He stared into her face – she looked as emotional as he felt.

This year Grace had made her own decoration for the tree. One that announced the arrival of her tiny baby brother. She was a proud big sister, and Matthew knew she would always look out for him.

Clara toddled over to her father wanting to be picked up. He squatted down and pulled her into his arms. Rose stood beside him, their tiny bundle of joy in her arms, wrapped warmly, ready to venture outside.

The kitten they'd welcomed into their home last Christmas rubbed up against his legs, and Grace leaned in and hugged her gently. Misty, named because of her grey color, didn't object.

Matthew's eyes darted around the room, taking it all in. His heart was full of joy. How could he have ever anticipated his life before Rose arrived?

Although she had endured great distress, they were both incredibly happy now, and so very much in love.

Matthew said a silent prayer to God for sending her to him.

"Can we have another kitten this year, Papa?" Grace asked as they began their trek toward the Christmas tree raising.

"No, Grace. One kitten is enough," he said firmly.

"Then can we have another baby next Christmas?" He glanced across at Rose. That was a wish he would gladly grant.

From the Author

Thank you so much for reading my book – I hope you enjoyed it.

I would greatly appreciate you leaving a review where you purchased, even if it is only a one-liner. It helps to have my books more visible!

About the Author

Multi-published, award-winning and bestselling author Cheryl Wright, former secretary, debt collector, account manager, writing coach, and shopping tour hostess, loves reading.

She writes historical romantic suspense and historical western romance.

She lives in Melbourne, Australia, and is married with two adult children and has six grandchildren, and twin great-grandchildren.

When she's not writing, she can be found in her craft room making greeting cards.

Links

Website: *http://www.cheryl-wright.com/*

Facebook Reader Group:
https://www.facebook.com/groups/cherylwrightaut hor/

Join My Newsletter:

https://cheryl-wright.com/newsletter/
(and receive a free book)